CROWING

IN

THE

DARK

RYAN STOUTE

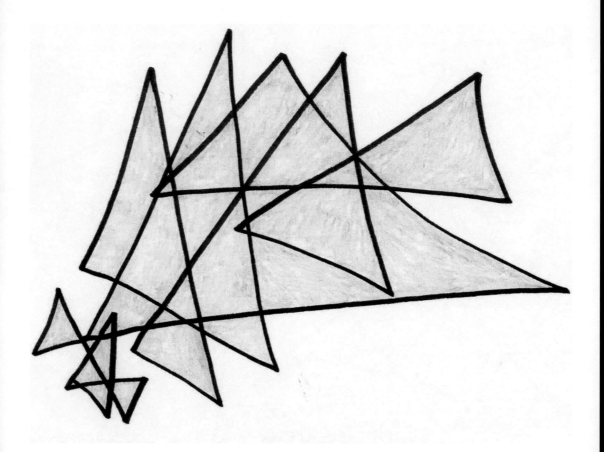

ENTERCESSORY

*Phannak, Ageless One, departed from the Abode of the Antiquities
to conquer the Predecessors.*

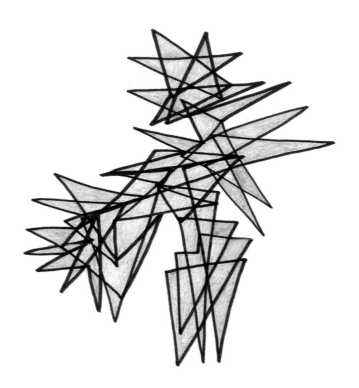

PHANNAK

And once he established control, the king-bird determined to place the domain in the hands of his two eldest sons.

PREDECESSORY

Nevertheless, the Predecessors denounced both Princes and refused to serve them; therefore, Phannak destroyed all with a mighty crowing roar.

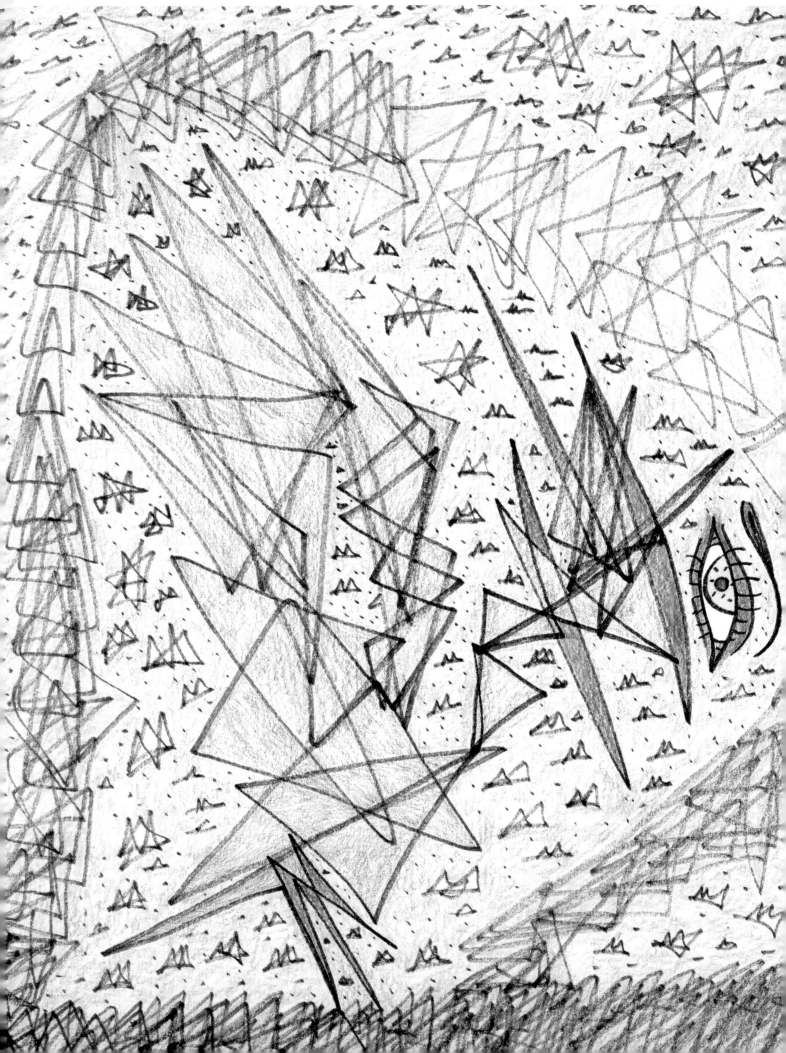

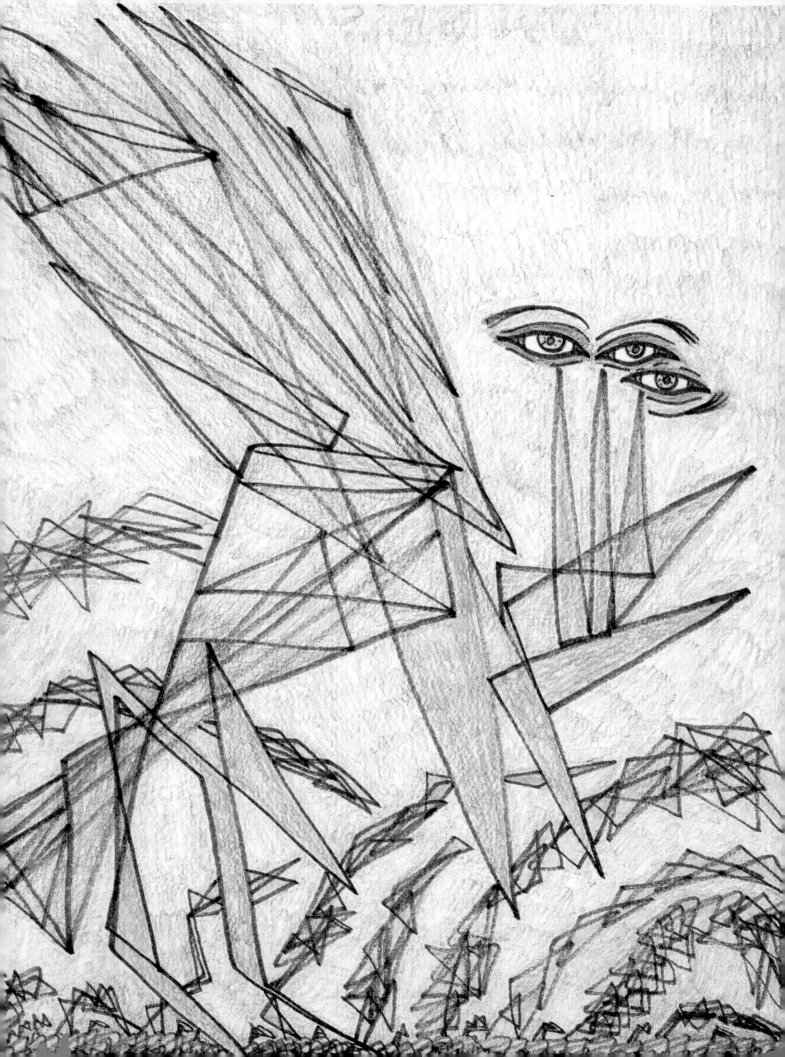

TRANSCESSORY

Then the Antiquity disclosed his reignless heirs.

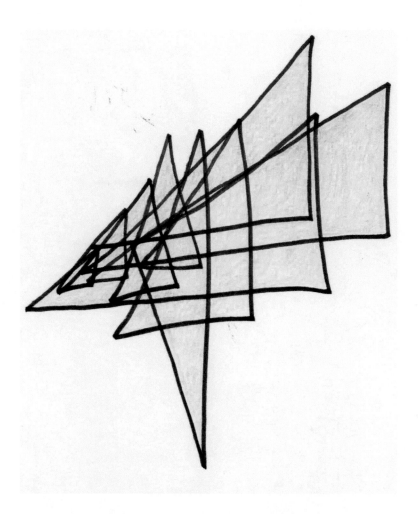

REENTERCESSORY

Regardless of their kinship, he removed them from his sight and delivered the unhaptics to the Intermediatory.

INTERCESSORY

SOKHIT AND SOKHEN

ANDEVI

Order this book online at www.trafford.com
or email orders@trafford.com

Most Trafford titles are also available at major online book retailers.

 www.trafford.com

North America & international
toll-free: 844 688 6899 (USA & Canada)
fax: 812 355 4082

Our mission is to efficiently provide the world's finest, most comprehensive book publishing service, enabling every author to experience success. To find out how to publish your book, your way, and have it available worldwide, visit us online at www.trafford.com

Because of the dynamic nature of the Internet, any web addresses or links contained in this book may have changed since publication and may no longer be valid. The views expressed in this work are solely those of the author and do not necessarily reflect the views of the publisher, and the publisher hereby disclaims any responsibility for them.

Any people depicted in stock imagery provided by Getty Images are models,
and such images are being used for illustrative purposes only.
Certain stock imagery © Getty Images.

ISBN: 978-1-4269-0406-6 (sc)

Library of Congress Control Number: 2010903775

Print information available on the last page.

Trafford rev.03/08/2021

Printed in the United States
by Baker & Taylor Publisher Services